POCKET ·

Published by the Penguin Group
27 Wrights Lane, London W8 5TZ, England
Viking Penguin Inc., 40 West 23rd Street, New York, New York 10010, U.S.A.
Penguin Books Australia Ltd, Ringwood, Victoria, Australia
Penguin Books Canada Limited, 2801 John Street, Markham, Ontario, Canada L3R 1B4
Penguin Book (N.Z.) Ltd, 182–190 Wairau Road, Auckland 10, New Zealand
Penguin Books Ltd, Registered Offices: Harmondsworth, Middlesex, England

Puffin/Moonlight
First published in Great Britain in 1988 in Pocket Puffins by Puffin Books
in association with Moonlight Publishing Ltd,
131 Kensington Church Street, London W8
Originally published by William Morrow and Company, New York in 1984
Copyright © Claire Schumacher, 1984

Printed in Italy by La Editoriale Libraria

Nutty's
Christmas

by Claire Schumacher

POCKET PUFFINS

In a forest live a family of squirrels.
Father and Mother, Butty, Fluffy,
Foxy and...

where is Nutty?

Nutty likes to climb trees looking for pine-cones and nuts. He has to hurry to catch up with his family.

Today Mother Squirrel is worried.
"The woodcutters are in our forest",
she warns the little squirrels.

"Stay away from the pine trees, and no climbing... Are you listening, Nutty? This means you, too!"

But Nutty has just spotted a beautiful pine-cone. *I'll just hop up and take it*, thinks Nutty.

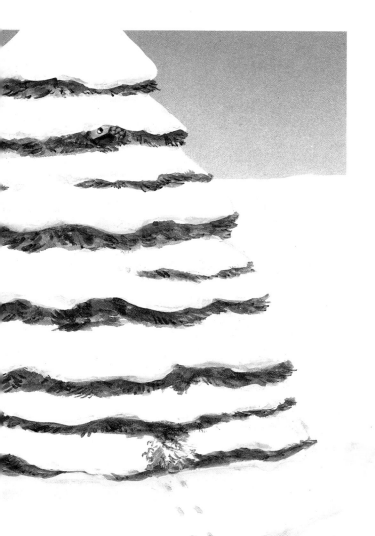

Nutty doesn't know that someone
else is looking at his tree.

The tree is falling down.
Nutty's eyes fill up with snow and
tears.

Far away from his family, Nutty hears little voices calling, "Here it is! Here comes the Christmas tree!"

Inside his tree, Nutty tells himself,
"Mummy is going to come and get
  me in a second."
But she doesn't.

In the forest, Nutty's family is calling to him.

"Look," says Foxy, "Nutty's feet are printed in the snow."

"Oh, my dear little Nutty",
sobs Mother Squirrel.

Nutty is still hidden deep inside his tree. He is afraid to move.

Nutty sees little hands putting shiny balls

and sparkling flowers on the branches.

"Hurry up, children, or we
will be late to pick up Grandma.
You, Brownie, stay outside
and guard the house."

As soon as the room
is quiet, Nutty jumps
out of the tree.

What funny flowers, thinks Nutty, tearing at the ribbons on the packages. They don't smell at all.

But a bottle of water smells like spring in the forest. Nutty opens up more packages and finds...

ME

M

... a car just his size.

Delicious smells
remind Nutty that
he hasn't eaten since
before the storm.

He jumps on the table and…

... tries a little bit of everything.

But a sudden noise
sends him scurrying
back to his tree.

"Who opened my packages?"
"Who tasted my biscuits and
threw nutshells all over the floor?"

"What's wrong, Brownie?"

Poor Nutty!

It's a good thing the doll's house window is too small for Brownie's nose.

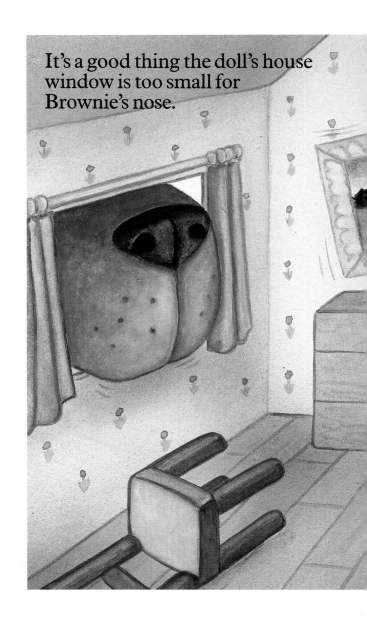

"Now we know who made this mess", says Father. "Can we keep him?" beg the children. But Mother says, "We cannot let him spend Christmas lost and scared."

In the forest Nutty's family is still looking for him. The truck frightens them, but imagine their surprise when out jumps...

"Nutty, dear Nutty, it's so good to see you."
"It's good to be home."

The End

CLAIRE SCHUMACHER was born and brought up in France. Her early years were spent in Normandy with five brothers and sisters. She studied at the Ecole Nationale Supérieure des Arts Décoratifs in Paris, and then worked as an illustrator in France for a while before moving to New York, where she now lives. As well as illustrating picture books, she has worked on a number of American magazines. *Nutty's Christmas* was her third children's picture book. She has written and illustrated several others since.

More Pocket Puffins for you to enjoy!

1. Picture books for reading aloud

Peter and the Wolf by Sergei Prokofiev and Erna Voigt
The well-known musical tale, beautifully illustrated.

This Little Pig-A-Wig by Lenore and Erik Blegvad
A lovely, lively collection of pig-poems old and new.

Wake Up, Bear...It's Christmas! by Stephen Gammell
Bear is determined not to sleep through the Christmas fun he's heard so much about.

There's a Nightmare in my Cupboard by Mercer Mayer
A hilarious, reassuring monster tale to tame any nightmare.

The Little Hare Book by Janosch
Stories, poems, jokes and riddles – a whole hare festival of fun and wit.

ABC Zoo by Sarah Matthews and Detlef Kersten
Delightful drawings transform letters into animals, enhanced by mischievous verses.

Walk, Rabbit, Walk by Elizabeth Attenborough and Colin McNaughton
Eagle has invited his friends to his mountain-top home for tea. Who will get there first?

2. Picture books for the early reader

Billy Goat and His Well-Fed Friends by Nonny Hogrogian
Billy Goat doesn't want to end up as the Farmer's supper...

The Pearl by Helme Heine
Beaver realises that there are greater riches in life than even the loveliest of pearls.

If I Had... by Mercer Mayer
'If only I had a gorilla, a crocodile, a snake... then no one would pick on me!' A little boy's daydreams find a real-life answer.

King Rooster, Queen Hen by Anita Lobel
Rooster and Hen set out to be King and Queen in the big city,
but meet crafty Fox, with almost disastrous results.

Bill and Stanley by Helen Oxenbury
A busy afternoon for Bill and his best friend,
the mildly eccentric dog Stanley.

Santa's Crash–Bang Christmas
by Steven Kroll and
Tomie de Paola
A very clumsy Father Christmas brings
havoc to a peaceful house.

Hurry Home, Grandma!
by Arielle North Olson and
Lydia Dabcovich
Will Grandma, the dauntless explorer,
make it home from the jungle in time
to help decorate the Christmas tree?

The Bear's Bicycle
by Emilie Warren McLeod and David McPhail
The hair-raising adventures of the bumbling bear
make a funny introduction to the rules of road safety.

Tough Eddie by Elizabeth Winthrop and Lillian Hoban
There is more to tough-guy Eddie than meets the eye…

3. Picture books for the more confident reader

The Twenty Elephant Restaurant
by Russell Hoban and Quentin Blake
A gloriously funny romp from this award-winning team.

Jack and the Beanstalk by Tony Ross
A lively new version of the traditional tale.

Puss in Boots by Tony Ross
Another traditional fairy tale re-told in
Tony Ross' inimitable style.

Fat Pig by Colin McNaughton
Fat Pig must lose weight.
Somehow his friends have to help him.

The Feathered Ogre by Lee Lorenz
Little Jack the Piper outwits the ferocious ogre and
plucks his golden feathers. A very funny fairy tale.

Mr Potter's Pigeon by Patrick Kinmonth and
Reg Cartwright
The touching story of an old man and his pet racing pigeon;
award-winning pictures.

The Little Moon Theatre by Irene Haas
A troupe of travelling players makes wishes come true.

Cully Cully and the Bear by Wilson Gage and
James Stevenson
Cully Cully the hunter wants a bearskin to lie on,
but the bear has other ideas.

Bob and Bobby by Tomie de Paola
Grandfather has a stroke, but is helped back to health by Bobby.
Illness and fear are no match for their direct and loving relationship.

Two Admirals by David McKee
David McKee's hilarious story of two vain admirals
and the chaos their rivalry brings to the village.

The Pigs' Wedding by Helme Heine
A day full of surprises, fun and happiness for
Trotter and Curlytail.

Hare and Badger Go To Town
by Naomi Lewis and Tony Ross
When Hare and Badger find their fields devastated with chemical
sprays, they think that life can only be better in the city.

A Child is Born by Jindra Čapek
A touching retelling of the traditional story of Christmas.